KU-216-527

First edition

Published by Ladybird Books Ltd Loughborough Leicestershire UK

© 1991 The Walt Disney Company
Printed in England (3)

WINNIE THE POOH
and Tigger too

Ladybird Books

Christopher Robin and Pooh

Once there was a boy called Christopher Robin. He was seven years old, and his best friend was a bear called Winnie the Pooh, or Pooh for short.

Pooh and his friends – Piglet, Rabbit, Eeyore the donkey, and bouncy Tigger –

all lived in a wonderful place called the Hundred Acre Wood. Grown ups said that they were only stuffed toys, but Christopher Robin knew better.

Pooh and his friends had lots of extraordinary adventures. The one you're going to hear about now happened not so very long ago...

One morning, Winnie the Pooh woke up feeling cheerful. When he looked out of the window and saw what a sunny day it was, he felt even more cheerful. And when Pooh felt cheerful, he liked to make up songs. First he sang a little song about himself:

"Winnie the Pooh, Winnie the Pooh,
Tubby little cubby all stuffed with fluff,
I'm Winnie the Pooh, Winnie the Pooh,
Willy-nilly silly old Bear!"

And then, because his favourite thing in all the world was honey, Pooh sang a little honey song:

"Isn't it funny
How a Bear likes honey?
Buzz! Buzz! Buzz!
I wonder why he does?"

Pooh was certain that the only reason bees made honey was so that *he* could eat it!

Pooh *did* eat a lot of honey. Most days he had honey for breakfast, lunch and tea. And he always had a Little Something for elevenses and another Little Something at bedtime.

Now, because Pooh ate so much honey, he was inclined to be a bit fat. So he had to do his Stoutness Exercises every morning. And when he did his Stoutness Exercises, he liked to have a good think.

But on this particular morning, he was having a hard time remembering what he was supposed to be thinking about.

"Oh, bother!" said Pooh. "I am a Bear of Very Little Brain. Maybe it will help if I start the day all over again."

So Pooh put on his nightshirt and nightcap again. He was just about to get back into bed, so that he could get up again, when...

Tigger Bounces In

...the door flew open, and in bounced Tigger.

"Hallooo!" said Tigger,

bouncing straight at Pooh.

"Goodness me!" gasped Pooh. "You startled me!"

"It's me, Tigger. T-I-G-G-E-R!"

"I know who you are. You've bounced on me before," said Pooh.

"Who are *you*?" asked Tigger.

"Why, Pooh, of course!" said Pooh.

"What's a Pooh?" asked Tigger, bouncing onto Pooh's tummy.

"You're sitting on one!" said Pooh. "And I must say, it's very uncomfortable!"

"Sorry!" said Tigger, bouncing off.

Suddenly Tigger caught sight of
something in Pooh's mirror. It was a
strange-looking animal with stripes and
a big nose. He tried to look fierce, but
the other animal just looked fiercer.

"Pooh, help!" Tigger shouted. He
was really frightened now.

Honey always made Pooh feel better, so he gave Tigger some honey to calm him down. But Tigger took one taste and made a face.

"Yuk!" he said. "Tiggers don't like this icky, sticky stuff!"

When Tigger looked in the mirror
again, he realised that the strange
animal was only his own reflection. He
quickly forgot all about being frightened
and bounced straight back at Pooh.

"I'm Tigger!" he shouted.
"T-I-G-G-"

"I know, I know!" said Pooh.
"Haven't you done enough bouncing
for one morning?"

"It's just my way of being friendly,"
said Tigger.

"Sitting on your friends doesn't seem
very friendly to me!" said Pooh.

"Oh well," said Tigger. "I suppose
I'll have to bounce at someone else,
then. Ta-ta for now!"

"Goodbye," said Pooh. "Tiggers are
certainly *tiring* animals," he thought to
himself. "Now where did I leave that
honey pot?"

Tigger went to see Piglet next.

"Halloo!" he said, bouncing at Piglet. Piglet was very small, and just one bounce was enough to knock him right over.

"Oh, Tigger, you frightened me!" said Piglet. "I wish you wouldn't do that."

"That was only a little bounce," said Tigger. "I'm saving my big bounces for Rabbit."

"Oh, in that case, thank you," said Piglet. But by then Tigger was on his way to Rabbit's house.

A Visit To Rabbit

Rabbit was working in his garden. Today he was busy with the carrots. Carrots were Rabbit's favourite food and he always grew plenty, so he'd have enough to last the winter. He was very proud of his garden, and of his fine crop.

Besides carrots, Rabbit liked beetroot and cabbage, and he was very fond of honey and condensed milk. He also liked his friends, Pooh and Piglet — except when Pooh ate too much of his honey and condensed milk. In fact, one of the only things Rabbit *didn't* like was being bounced at by Tigger.

But what Tigger liked best of all was bouncing at Rabbit.

"Hallooo, Rabbit!" called Tigger. He bounced right into Rabbit's garden,

knocking over everything in sight. "It's me, Tigger. T-I-G-"

"Don't bother spelling it!" said Rabbit crossly. "And *don't* bounce all over my garden! Just look at it!"

"Yuk! Messy, isn't it?" said Tigger.

"Messy?" screeched Rabbit. "*Messy*? It's ruined! And it's all your fault! Why don't you *ever* stop bouncing?"

"Because," said Tigger, "bouncing is what Tiggers do best." And he sang Rabbit his special song:

"The wonderful thing about Tiggers
Is Tiggers are wonderful things!
Their tops are made out of rubber,
Their bottoms are made out of springs.
They're bouncy, trouncy, flouncy,
pouncy,

Fun, fun, fun, fun, fun!
But the most wonderful thing about
Tiggers

Is I'm the only one!"

Rabbit Calls a Meeting

By the time Tigger bounced away, Rabbit was furious. "That bouncing has *got* to stop," he muttered to himself.

But Rabbit wasn't sure *how* to stop Tigger bouncing. He rummaged through his cupboards and drawers looking for something that might be helpful, but he couldn't find a thing. So he called a meeting and invited Pooh and Piglet.

"Friends," said Rabbit, when they were all together, "I'm sure you'll agree that Tigger is getting far too bouncy."

Pooh and Piglet nodded.

"It's time we taught him a lesson," Rabbit went on. "It's time we *un*bounced Tigger!"

"Yes," said Piglet, "but how?"

"My thoughts exactly," said Rabbit. "What do *you* think, Pooh?"

Pooh always got sleepy at meetings of

this sort, and he was having trouble
keeping his eyes open. When he heard
his name, he sat up with a start.

"Extremely!" he said.

"Extremely what?" said Rabbit.

"What you were saying," replied
Pooh. "Undoubtedly!"

"Pooh," said Piglet, "weren't you listening to Rabbit?"

"Of course I was," said Pooh. "I just have a small piece of fluff in my ear. Can you ask your question again, please, Rabbit?"

"Where should I start from, Pooh?"

"From whenever I got the fluff in my ear," said Pooh.

"When was that?" asked Rabbit.

"We were just wondering," said Piglet, who was getting impatient, "how we could unbounce Tigger."

Suddenly Rabbit had an idea. "I know!" he said. "We'll take Tigger on a Long Explore to somewhere he's never been, and we'll lose him!"

"Lose him?" said Piglet, sounding worried.

"Oh, we'll come back the next day and find him again," said Rabbit, "but by then he'll have learnt his lesson. He'll be a different Tigger – a humble Tigger,

a small and sorry Tigger – and he'll never bounce at us again! Now, all in favour of my plan say 'Aye'."

"Aye," said Piglet.

"Pooh?" said Rabbit.

Piglet nudged Pooh awake.

"Yes!" exclaimed Pooh. "Certainly! I..."

"Good!" said Rabbit. "Motion carried."

A Walk In the Forest

The next morning was cold and misty.

Rabbit was in such a hurry to get started that Pooh forgot to take a Little Something to eat on the way.

Tigger bounced on ahead of the others. He bounced farther and farther into the mist, until he disappeared.

"My plan is working!" said Rabbit.

"Is Tigger lost now?" asked Piglet.

"He will be soon," said Rabbit.
"And we'll be able to go home."

"Good," said Pooh. "It's nearly
lunchtime."

Suddenly they heard a voice in the mist. "Hallooo!" it called. It was Tigger!

"Quick!" said Rabbit. "He mustn't see us. Let's hide in that hollow tree trunk!"

"Hallooo!" Tigger called again. "Are you there, Rabbit? Pooh, Piglet, where are you?" Tigger was beginning to feel quite worried.

"We're here, of course," said Pooh,
trying to be helpful.

"Ssh! Keep quiet!" whispered Rabbit.
"You'll spoil everything!"

Tigger kept looking all round.
"That's funny," he said, jumping onto
the tree trunk. "I was sure they were
right behind me. Pooh! Piglet! Rabbit!
Say something!"

Then Tigger's tail got stuck in a crack
in the tree trunk. Pooh nearly said
something again, but Rabbit stopped
him just in time.

Tigger pulled his tail free and bounced
away into the mist, hoping to find his
friends.

"He's lost for sure now!" said
Rabbit. "Let's go home." He felt very
pleased with himself.

But soon Rabbit was feeling a lot less pleased. "You know," he said, as they passed a sandpit, "everywhere looks the same in the mist."

"That's because we've been past this sandpit before," said Pooh.

"We have?" said Rabbit. "Well, it's a good thing I know the forest so well. Otherwise we might get lost. Now, follow me!"

But no matter which way they went, the three friends always ended up in the same place.

By the time they had passed the sandpit five times, Pooh was tired of seeing it. Besides, his tummy was feeling very empty.

"I've had a Good Idea," said Pooh at last. "Why don't we walk away from the sandpit and then *try* to find it again?"

"Whatever for, Pooh?" asked Piglet.

"Well, if we keep finding the sandpit when we're trying to find home, maybe when we try to find *it*, we'll find home instead!"

"I don't see much sense in that," said Rabbit. "If I walk away from this sandpit and try to find it again, of *course* I'll find it. Just wait here and I'll show you."

And Rabbit walked off into the mist.

Pooh's Tummy Rumbles

Pooh and Piglet waited for Rabbit to come back. They waited and waited. They waited a very long time.

Pooh had plenty of time to think. And what he thought about was all the honey that was waiting for *him* in his cupboard at home.

Suddenly Piglet said, "Pooh, I just heard a funny noise!"

"That was my tummy rumbling," said Pooh. "It wants to go home even more than I do! Come on, let's go."

"But Pooh, do you know the way?" asked Piglet.

"No, but my tummy will find it," said Pooh. "There are twelve pots of honey in my cupboard, and they're all calling to my tummy. And just now my tummy answered them. All we have to do is to follow my tummy, and we'll be home in time for lunch."

So they set off. Pooh could hear the honey pots calling very clearly now, and Piglet kept very quiet so as not to interrupt them.

Soon the mist began to lift, and Pooh and Piglet saw where they were – and

 who was waiting for them.

"Hallooo, you two!" said Tigger. "Where have you been? I've looked *everywhere* for you!"

"Pooh," whispered Piglet, "I don't think Rabbit's plan worked!"

"We've just been finding the way home," Pooh told Tigger. "But I think we've lost Rabbit."

"Don't worry, I'll find him!" said Tigger. "See you soon!" And he bounced away into the forest.

Rabbit *was* lost. He was feeling a very small and sorry Rabbit indeed when he suddenly saw a familiar figure bouncing towards him.

"Tigger!" Rabbit gasped. "You're supposed to be lost!"

"Oh, Tiggers never get lost," said Tigger.

"Never?" asked Rabbit.

"Not ever," said Tigger. "Now let's go home." And he bounced back through the forest, with Rabbit following quietly and humbly behind him.

Rabbit and Tigger were soon friends again – nobody stays cross for very long in the Hundred Acre Wood.

But Rabbit did get a bit annoyed with Eeyore the donkey, because Eeyore told Christopher Robin all about Rabbit's plan. However, Rabbit and Eeyore soon made friends again.

Christopher Robin forgave Rabbit for being cross with Tigger, and Tigger promised to be more careful of where he bounced in future.

Pooh was happy to be home, of course, and went straight to his honey pots. He offered Piglet a Little Something as well, and the two of them had a lovely lunch that day.

And that is the end of this story about Tigger and Rabbit and Piglet and of course Winnie the Pooh.

There are many more stories, and many more friends to meet.

Grown ups think that all these stories are make-believe, and that Christopher Robin's friends are only stuffed toys. But you and I know better, don't we?

Of course we do – as sure as there's a Hundred Acre Wood!